P9-API-077

DATE DUE

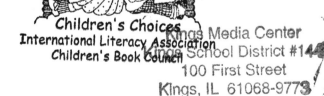

YOU CHOOSE BOOKS

Little Red Riding Hood

AN INTERACTIVE FAIRY TALE ADVENTURE

by Eric Braun

illustrated by
Mariano Epelbaum

CAPSTONE PRESS
a capstone imprint

You Choose Books are published by Capstone Press,
1710 Roe Crest Drive, North Mankato, Minnesota 56003
www.capstonepub.com

Library of Congress Cataloging-in-Publication Data
Braun, Eric, 1971– author.
Little Red Riding Hood: an interactive fairy tale adventure / by Eric Braun.
pages cm. — (You choose. Fractured fairy tales)
"You Choose Books."
Summary: In this You Choose adventure, Little Red Riding Hood can be a girl in an
urban park, a boy in the middle of a war, or the more traditional girl in the forest—
the choice is up to the reader.
ISBN 978-1-4914-5856-3 (library binding)
ISBN 978-1-4914-5929-4 (paperback)
ISBN 978-1-4914-5941-6 (ebook pdf)
1. Little Red Riding Hood (Tale)—Adaptations. 2. Plot-your-own stories. 3. Fairy
tales. [1. Fairy tales. 2. Plot-your-own stories.] I. Title.
PZ8.B6732Li 2016
[Fic]—dc23   2015004119

Editorial Credits
Kristen Mohn, editor; Ted Williams, designer; Nathan Gassman, creative director;
Tori Abraham, production specialist

Image Credits
Shutterstock: solarbird, background

Printed in Canada.
032015   008825FRF15

Table of Contents

About Your Adventure.......................... 4

CHAPTER 1
Alone in the Woods.................... .7

CHAPTER 2
Bad Reputation............................ 11

CHAPTER 3
Fleeing Through the Night........... 53

CHAPTER 4
Attack Plans.............................. 83

CHAPTER 5
A Little History on Little Red.... 107

Critical Thinking Using the Common Core............ 111

Read More 112

Internet Sites.. 112

ABOUT YOUR ADVENTURE

4

The woods are dark and deep. And they're easy to get lost in. Even worse, you sense there's something out there that means you harm.

In this fairy tale, you control your fate. Put on the cape of Little Red Riding Hood and make choices to determine what happens next.

Chapter One sets the scene. Then you choose which path to read. Follow the directions at the bottom of the page as you read the stories. The decisions you make will change your outcome. After you finish one path, go back and read the others for new perspectives and more adventures ... if you make it out of the woods.

5

Alone in the Woods

YOU are walking alone through a forest in the dark of night. A picnic basket trembles in your hand. You move quickly along the path, careful to avoid rocks and tree roots that seem to grab at your feet. The forest itself feels alive.

With one eye you scan the dark shadows between the trees. What moved in there? Was that a pair of eyes?

Where you come from, everyone is afraid of these woods—and so are you.

People say that children disappear in here. They say watch out for wolves in this forest—the wolves will try to trick you, scare you, take you. They say to never go into these woods alone, and never, ever go in at night.

Yet here you are. You wouldn't be if it wasn't so important. You must get to Grandmother. Everything depends on it.

After walking for some time, nothing bad happens, and you begin to relax. The stars are out. The owls hoot. It's not so scary, you think. It's actually kind of nice.

That's when you hear the voice: "Where are you going, child?"

TO BE A MODERN-DAY KID WALKING THROUGH A LARGE CITY PARK, TURN TO PAGE 11.

TO BE A CHILD CAUGHT IN A TERRIBLE WAR, TURN TO PAGE 53.

TO BE A FUTURISTIC AGENT WORKING AGAINST AN EVIL CORPORATION, TURN TO PAGE 83.

9

CHAPTER 2

Bad Reputation

The Fairy Tale wolves are angry. Lately, nice wolves have made news headlines for helping old ladies cross the street, volunteering at the children's hospital, and donating money to build new playgrounds. One wolf has even pledged to run around City Park 1,000 times to raise awareness for homeless people. The news stations have been all over that.

The wolves from "Peter and the Wolf," "The Boy Who Cried Wolf," "The Three Little Pigs," and "Little Red Riding Hood" have retired to the city to relax—but not to stop being bad. They can't stand by and watch these nice wolves ruin their hard-earned reputation for evildoing.

To restore their bad name, they have teamed up to terrorize citizens who go into the park at night. You have heard the tortured screams of the poor suckers who got caught in the park after dark.

Now you are one of those poor suckers.

Here's how it happened: Your grandmother got sick and asked you to bring her some milk and Yummy-Pops cereal—her favorite food—to cheer her up. You love hanging out with her. The two of you watch funny cat videos, knit hilarious finger puppets, and eat bowl after bowl of cereal. You especially love the stories of her brave adventures sailing a stormy ocean, climbing a towering mountain, and outwitting burglars. She even survived an encounter with three bears when she was a girl.

Unfortunately, she lives on the other side of the park. Even though the park is scary, you couldn't say no to Grandmother. The park stretches for miles. Going around it takes hours. Better to just run through it quickly and get it over with. Besides, you need to toughen up, like Grandma.

But now that a wolf is standing in front of you, you wish you had at least waited until morning. He leans against a lamppost and uses a gleaming white fang to clean out the mud (or is it blood?) from underneath one of his long, sharp claws. A silver stripe of fur runs from his nose to his tail.

With a trembling hand, you remove your earbuds. "What did you say?"

"Where are you going, child?"

TO MAKE A RUN FOR IT, TURN TO PAGE 14.

TO TRY TO TALK YOUR WAY OUT OF THIS, TURN TO PAGE 16.

You run toward the gated entrance to the forest, not far ahead. Surely the wolf won't chase you into the well-lit street.

"What do you fear?" the wolf says behind you. Right behind you. Like, in your ear. He's quick.

Panting to catch your breath, you turn and look into his yellow eyes. Grandmother would not be afraid, and it angers you that you're being a chicken. Besides, you think of the news reports. Maybe this is one of those good wolves. "I'm not afraid," you say.

The wolf's lips stretch back into a wide, toothy grin. "Of course," he purrs. "But you should be afraid. This park is full of bad wolves. We good wolves can only do so much to protect people. You shouldn't be here alone."

"You're a good wolf?" you ask, your voice trembling.

"Child," the wolf says, "if I were a big bad wolf, would you not be eaten up by now?"

He makes a good point. But still, something about this wolf makes the hairs on your arm stand up. You pull up your hood and say, "Well, I better go."

"Better come with me," he says. "I'll keep you safe … from the bad wolves."

TO FOLLOW THE WOLF, TURN TO PAGE 19.

TO LEAVE HIM, TURN TO PAGE 22.

15

"I am going to visit my grandmother," you say to Stripe, the wolf. "I'm late, so if you don't mind, I'll be going now."

Stripe lets out a low growl. "I do mind," he says. "You don't get to come through this park at night without paying a price." He cleans another claw on his fang and scrapes it along the lamppost to sharpen it. You've seen similar claw marks around the park, like graffiti.

"W-w-what price?" you ask.

Stripe reaches a hairy arm toward you, and his claws gleam in the lamplight. Saliva drips from his open jaws. You back away.

"Wait!" you say, thinking fast. "I know how you can get rid of all those nice wolves. Those goody-two-shoes wolves deserve to be punished!" you holler, slamming your fist into your hand.

Stripe lowers his paw. "Keep talking, kid," he says.

You look both ways as if about to tell a huge secret. "I know where wolfsbane grows," you say quietly. "I just have to drop off this cereal with my grandmother first, and then I'll meet you back here."

17

TURN THE PAGE.

The wolf's eyes get big. "Do you know how many good wolves I can kill with a poison like that?" he asks excitedly. But then his eyes narrow again. "How do I know you'll come back?" he says.

"We'll exchange cell phone numbers," you say, pulling out your phone. You're not sure if the wolf believes your story.

TO RUN FOR IT, TURN TO PAGE 23.

TO EXCHANGE CELL PHONE NUMBERS, TURN TO PAGE 24.

"OK, thanks," you say. If the evil wolves are even creepier than this wolf, you don't want to meet them.

"Excellent," the wolf purrs, taking you by the hand with his hairy paw. He leads you off the path into the trees. The yellow eyes of other wolves glow in the darkness. Something inside your head starts to wail like a siren. This was a mistake! You try to wrench your hand away, but the wolf holds tight.

"Let me go!" you scream.

"Yes, let the child go!" says a hoarse voice. You twist around to see another wolf loping toward you—a good wolf!

19

TURN THE PAGE.

You feel the striped wolf release your hand.

"Run!" the good wolf yells. You scramble to

your feet and sprint toward the park exit. You

hear the terrible, snarling sounds of the two

wolves fighting.

You leave the park and run quickly to Grandmother's apartment. As you approach the building, you see a man with a badge carrying a rifle toward the park. He's one of the new "wolf patrolmen" who have been working to protect people from the bad wolves. As you stop to tell him what happened, you think you see a wolf creeping in the shadows on the street.

The patrolman runs into the park to investigate. You push the button for your grandmother's unit, and a scratchy voice croaks through the speaker: "Who is it?"

Grandmother sounds really sick! "Little Red," you say, and she buzzes you up. When you get to her apartment, the door is open just slightly. That's unusual—she always keeps it locked.

TO PEEK INSIDE, TURN TO PAGE 26.

TO WALK IN, TURN TO PAGE 28.

You begin to walk away but the wolf steps in front of you. "You're not going anywhere," he says.

Just as you suspected: He's an evil Fairy Tale wolf—not one of the good wolves. Your only hope is to distract him. "Look!" you say, pointing into the trees. "That nice wolf is picking up trash in the park!"

"What?" the wolf says, following your gaze. "I hate those guys!"

While he's looking away, you turn and sprint for the park exit. You throw the picnic basket back at the wolf, who is now hot on your tracks. He's so close you can smell his dog breath.

Just outside the gate, you see the shadow of a tall man with a rifle.

TO CALL OUT FOR HELP, TURN TO PAGE 30.

TO KEEP RUNNING, TURN TO PAGE 32.

22

You wait for the wolf to put his hand into his own pocket to fish out his phone. When he does, you turn and bolt for the park gate.

You hear the wolf's phone thunk to the ground and the swift patter of his paws as he comes after you. You hear his breathing—or is that your breathing? You soon realize you're hearing the panting of an entire pack of wolves. The Fairy Tale wolves have teamed up to share in the pleasure of gobbling you up.

You wish you really did have some wolfsbane.

THE END

TO FOLLOW ANOTHER PATH, TURN TO PAGE 9.

You tell the wolf a made-up cell number. You feel your temples drip with sweat, but you try to act natural. The wolf watches as you attempt to casually walk away. When you reach the edge of the park, you run out onto a bustling city street with relief.

Near the entrance to Grandma's building, a man wearing a badge holds a rifle to his shoulder. He winks at you as you enter the building. You don't recognize him.

You press the button for Grandma's apartment, but there's no reply. You press it again. Finally Grandmother's scratchy voice comes over the intercom. "Who is it?"

"It's me, Grandma."

She buzzes open the door, and you walk upstairs to her third-floor apartment. You find the bedroom door open with grandma lying in bed. The blankets are pulled up over her head.

You sniff the air. What is that smell? After a second, you recognize it: Stripe. He's here somewhere.

TO STAY IN THE DOORWAY FOR A QUICK ESCAPE, TURN TO PAGE 33.

TO GO IN TO SEE GRANDMOTHER, TURN TO PAGE 37.

You peek inside and see "Stripe," the wolf. He's slinking in through an open window and across the floor toward your grandmother's bed! As you're watching, he lifts her up with his meaty paws and devours her in one bite. It happens so quickly, you don't even have time to scream.

Stripe, still swallowing the massive, fighting lump of Grandma, turns and sees you. He gulps, saliva dripping off his hairy chin. You can't believe he's still hungry, but he's looking at you with a gleam in his eye that tells you he is.

Stripe belches and picks one of your grandmother's slippers out from between his teeth. "Come, child," he growls.

You look around. You don't see anything that could be used as a weapon except maybe Grandmother's walker—you could whack him with it.

27

Maybe you should run down the stairs. Stripe is full and fat, now. He might not be able to catch you. You think: What would Grandmother do?

TO RUN AWAY, TURN TO PAGE 39.

TO FIGHT THE WOLF, TURN TO PAGE 42.

You walk in. There in the living room is Stripe the wolf, snarling at Grandmother. When he sees you, he says, "Excellent, now I get to eat you both."

"Not if we can help it," Grandmother says, taking advantage of the distraction you made.

Stripe leaps toward her, but in a surprising blur, she whacks him across the muzzle with something. She smiles and holds up the baseball bat from her days on the first women's major league team.

"All right, Grandma!" you say as Stripe flops to the floor.

But then he gets back up, his own blood staining his lips. As Stripe slinks toward Grandma, he shoves you to the floor and you bang your head on the fireplace. You watch as Grandma swings the bat again, but this time Stripe is ready. He catches the bat in his great mouth and crunches down, splintering the wood. You and Grandma exchange a horrified look.

Gums bleeding and full of splinters, Stripe turns on Grandma. This time, it looks like he's going in for the kill. You don't know what to do.

TO MAKE ONE LAST ATTACK ON THE WOLF, TURN TO PAGE 45.

TO PLAY DEAD AND HOPE HE LEAVES YOU ALONE, TURN TO PAGE 47.

29

"Help!" you holler. The man lifts his rifle to his shoulder and points it behind you, but then he lowers it again. You realize the footsteps behind you have stopped. You reach the rifleman and stop to rest, panting.

You look back into the park, but the wolf is nowhere to be seen.

"Thank you," you say. "You scared him away. He was going to ..." But the man runs off without a word. Is he pursuing the wolf? You don't stick around to find out. You hurry across the busy street to Grandmother's building and press the button for her apartment. She buzzes you in.

You find her lying in bed with the covers over her head. She must really be sick.

"I'm sorry, Grandma," you call into the room. "I lost the cereal. I threw it at a wolf that was chasing me."

"It's okay, dear," Grandmother says weakly. "I really just wanted to see you."

Just then there's a loud knock at the door. A deep voice says, "Open up—quick!"

Grandmother struggles to sit up in bed. "Let him in!" she says.

TO OPEN THE DOOR, **TURN TO PAGE 48.**

TO FIND OUT WHO IT IS FIRST, **TURN TO PAGE 50.**

You run harder toward the gate, gasping for breath. The wolf's bounding steps close in behind you.

Just as you're about to escape, you feel sharp claws dig into your shoulders. You crumple to the ground. You hear a piercing howl and realize that it's coming from you.

Your shredded back and shoulders ignite with pain. The wolf's saliva drips into your ear, and his knifelike teeth sink into your neck. You hear a rifle shot and the yelp of the wolf as he's hit. Then you feel the weight of him collapse upon you.

32

The man with the rifle rushes up to you, but the look on his face tells you there's no hope. Your howl turns into a moan, and then everything is silent.

THE END

TO FOLLOW ANOTHER PATH, TURN TO PAGE 9.

"Grandmother," you call from the doorway. "Are you okay?"

"I'm okay," she calls back. "One of those kind wolves was here delivering groceries. Can you smell him?"

You relax. "So that's what I smell," you say. You walk into her bedroom. But lying there in her dark bedroom, she doesn't look right. "Grandmother," you say, "what big eyes you've got."

"Yes, dear," she replies. "The better to see you with."

33

You step closer and see her hand on top of the blanket. "And what large hands you've got."

"The better to hug you with."

TURN THE PAGE.

"My goodness, Grandmother, what big, hairy ears you've got."

"The better to hear your sweet voice, my dear." Grandmother smiles, showing all her teeth.

"And what big teeth …" you whisper.

"Those," Grandmother says, lowering the blanket and setting foot—or paw—to the floor, "are all the better to eat you with!"

You run out of the bedroom just as the man carrying the rifle bursts in. You cower on the floor and hear a loud bang. When you open your eyes, 34 you see Stripe lying dead on the floor.

The man grabs a long knife from the kitchen and slices open the wolf's stomach. He reaches into the bloody guts and pulls Grandma out by the wrists. She comes up gasping for air.

TURN THE PAGE.

While Grandmother gets cleaned up, you talk with the man over bowls of Yummy-Pops. He's a Wolf Watch officer—part of a nonprofit organization set up to protect citizens from bad wolves. "I saw you come out of the park," he says. "I knew there would be a wolf following you."

"Thank goodness you saw me," you say.

"Now," the man says. "Do you want to know where the wolfsbane really is?"

You nod. No more wolves will push you around.

THE END

TO FOLLOW ANOTHER PATH, TURN TO PAGE 9.

As soon as you walk in, you realize something is wrong—very wrong. Grandmother is nowhere to be seen, but Stripe is standing by the bed putting on her pajamas.

"What the heck are you doing?" you say.

"Digesting a nice dinner," the wolf says calmly.

"Where's Grandmother?"

"I knew that phone number you gave me was fake, kid, so I followed you here. While you waited in the lobby, I climbed the fire escape."

"Where's Grandmother?" you repeat.

"Such a lovely woman," Stripe says. "And so delicious."

TURN THE PAGE.

You turn to run, but the wolf is quicker. With both paws he lifts you high over his gaping mouth, then lowers you headfirst down his throat. The saliva coats you, and his slimy throat muscles contract and pull your head down as he shoves your legs deeper into his mouth with his fists.

You throw elbows and try to kick, but you can't move. It's like being in an extremely tight, slippery sleeping bag. You can't breathe. Just as you are about to black out, you feel a wrinkly hand grab hold of yours. At least you and Grandmother will go down together.

38

THE END

TO FOLLOW ANOTHER PATH, TURN TO PAGE 9.

No way can you fight a wolf—you're just a kid! You remember the patrolman. You turn and race down the stairs, two at a time. Stripe's snarls echo in the stairwell behind you.

When you reach the street, you see the patrolman with two good wolves. Stripe barges out of the door behind you. You start to duck in case there will be any shooting, but then you stop. "Don't shoot him in the stomach! He ate Grandmother!" you yell out.

Stripe dives on the patrolman, knocking the rifle from his hands. The other two wolves try to pull him off, but Stripe bucks them off. The four of them fight for a few minutes, grunts and blood everywhere. Eventually the man rolls out from under the pack and takes aim at Stripe. He pulls the trigger, but it only clicks.

39

TURN THE PAGE.

Stripe springs to his hind legs and gives the patrolman a mighty shove in the chest with both paws. The man falls backward over a car and lands with a sickening thud.

Stripe wipes blood from his lips. "Look at you two!" he says to the other wolves, who are cowering injured on the ground. "You should be ashamed! That man would have killed you. But you helped him! You run around shoveling snow for senior citizens and giving candy to babies. YOU ARE WOLVES! Act like it!"

All three wolves are breathing hard and **40** bleeding. The two "good" wolves look at you with a glint in their eyes.

"Show some self-respect," Stripe says. He rubs his stomach. "I've got a belly full of grandma, and it feels great! You should try it." The other two wolves narrow their eyes at you. Then all three approach. It's only a question of which will get to you first.

THE END

TO FOLLOW ANOTHER PATH, TURN TO PAGE 9.

Grandma always did the courageous thing.
You know that she would fight. You dash toward
her reclining chair, grab her metal walker, and lift
it over your head. Then you bring it down hard
on Stripe's muzzle.

"Ooof!" the wolf says, staggering.

Encouraged, you do it again, but the second hit doesn't seem to hurt him as much. Stripe looks up at you and laughs.

"You'll be a tasty morsel," Stripe says, fogging you with his terrible breath.

You raise the walker again, but while it's above your head, Stripe lunges. He slashes you across the belly with his razor-sharp claws. Your red hoodie is shredded, and blood seeps into the fabric. Stripe slashes again but you hook his paw in the walker. You twist, turning his paw at a painful angle. Stripe yowls in pain and looks up at you with big, bulging eyes. "My, what big eyes you have," you whisper to him as you push him backward right out the window and onto the pavement far below.

43

TURN THE PAGE.

You get a big knife from the kitchen, run down to the street, and cut open the wolf's belly. Grandmother crawls out. She coughs and spits, and after a few seconds she stands up and hugs you.

"He said he was a good wolf here with my milk delivery," she says, shaking her head. Then she whispers in your ear, "Thank you. This will be one to tell *your* grandkids."

THE END

TO FOLLOW ANOTHER PATH, TURN TO PAGE 9.

You have no weapons, but you can't give up when Grandmother is about to be eaten. You grope around for anything to hit Stripe with and find a throw pillow. You swat the wolf with it. *Thwap!*

Stripe looks at you in disbelief, then blinks a couple times as puffs of dust surround him. Suddenly a massive sneeze storms from his maw. Saliva, snot, and a little blood spew out. Again, you whack Stripe with the pillow. More dust puffs into his face.

"Knock it off!" he says, rubbing his nose and sneezing some more.

45

You keep hitting him. Dust floats in the air like fog. Wow, Grandmother sure doesn't clean very often! Stripe collapses to the floor in a sneezing fit. He blows his nose on the rug, tears running down his face.

TURN THE PAGE.

You lunge for the walker. You lift it high, then bring it down hard on Stripe's head. The sneezing stops for good.

You rush over to check Grandma's pulse. It is weak, but she's alive. You call 911. The paramedics who arrive are good wolves who have devoted their lives to helping others.

"Put her on the platter," one of them says, as they pick up Grandmother. "I mean the stretcher," he corrects himself, looking at you nervously.

"Are you sure you're good wolves?" you ask.

46 "Old habits die hard," the wolf says.

THE END

TO FOLLOW ANOTHER PATH, TURN TO PAGE 9.

Your only hope is to play dead. You lay as still as possible, barely breathing, as Stripe tears into Grandmother. You are forced to listen to her shrieks and "ows!" along with the wolf's rude chewing sounds as you wait.

Finally you hear him belch and sigh. Then his claws click across the floor toward you. You realize you were a fool to think he'd leave you alone. You should have at least tried to fight. Instead, you're going to be dessert.

THE END

TO FOLLOW ANOTHER PATH, TURN TO PAGE 9.

47

You open the door to the tall man with the rifle. "It's you," you say. He pushes in, then shuts and bolts the door.

"Hello, Albert," Grandmother croaks.

"Hello, Granny," he says. "I just got a call from the three little pigs, and they say the wolves are huffing and puffing again. That brick house is going down tonight unless we do something. I was hoping you could help."

"I just don't have the energy for a fight tonight. But maybe my grandchild can help?"

48   "M-m-me?" you stammer. "I just got away from the wolves, I'm not going back out there!" But you don't want to let down Grandmother, so you agree to help. Albert puts a rifle in your trembling hands and leads you to the brick house of the pigs. There you see several wolves huffing and puffing in unison. The house buckles under the gales but holds.

You and Albert raise your rifles and shoot at the same time. Two of the wolves drop dead, and the other two run. The house is safe.

"Thank you!" one of the pigs hollers, waving a hoof. You feel exhilarated! You realize that you might have a bit of your grandmother's courage in you after all.

THE END

TO FOLLOW ANOTHER PATH, TURN TO PAGE 9.

What if it's the wolf? Better to be safe. You pick up Grandma's lucky baseball bat and call out, "Who's there?"

"It's Albert. Let me in!" the voice says.

"How can we be sure it's you?" you ask.

"Oh, no!" he yells.

"What?" you yell back.

"Let him in, child!" Grandmother says desperately.

You open the door a crack and peer out to see the man with the badge from the park firing his rifle down the stairs. A wolf on the stairs collapses, but two others approach.

The man tries to reload his gun, but one of the wolves leaps up the stairs and pounces on him. You slam the door and lock it. Screams, growls, and howls come through the shaking walls.

"Was it Albert?" Grandmother says. "The man with the rifle? He is coming to help us get rid of the wolves."

You lean against the door, realizing your hesitation cost Albert his life. Even worse, the wolves will be bursting into Grandmother's apartment at any moment.

51

THE END

TO FOLLOW ANOTHER PATH, TURN TO PAGE 9.

CHAPTER 3

Fleeing Through the Night

You have never seen your parents so scared. They pulled you out of bed in the middle of the night, gave you a small basket of food, and brought you to this path at the edge of the woods. Wanting to stay hidden, they don't light a lantern. It is very dark.

"They are coming," your father says. You know who he means: the Soldiers. They are coming to take the children away. You, your family, your friends, and everyone in your village have been worrying about this for weeks.

53

"Walk quickly along this path," your father says, "and do not stop until you reach the village on the far side of the forest. If you walk fast, you will arrive mid-morning tomorrow. The town is called Bon Jardin."

He tells you that when you reach the town, a kind, grandmotherly woman named Simone will be waiting for you in the first small cottage you reach. She will feed you and hide you from the Soldiers. She has hidden many children. You can trust Simone—and only Simone. "Avoid anyone else," your father says. "If anyone stops you, tell them that you are bringing a cake to your sick grandmother."

You hug your father and mother, who is weeping softly. "When will I see you?" you ask.

"Soon," your mother promises. But she doesn't sound very sure. How can she be? Nobody can predict what will happen during war.

"Hurry now," your father says. You do as you are told and dash into the woods with only faint starlight to guide you.

For several hours you are alone and your fears settle. But suddenly a twig snaps in the trees, and you freeze. A deep voice asks, "Where are you going, child?" A Soldier steps out of the woods.

TO RUN AWAY FROM HIM ALONG THE PATH, TURN TO PAGE 56.

TO TELL HIM THAT YOU'RE BRINGING CAKE TO YOUR GRANDMOTHER, TURN TO PAGE 58.

You're small and fast. You think you can lose him, so you run.

"Stop!" he says. "Or the penalty will be severe!"

It will be severe if I *do* stop, you think. You can hear his gear jangling as he runs after you. A beam of light sweeps across the path. You're faster than he is and soon you're able to gain some distance. But you're growing tired.

"Stop!" he yells again—his voice is far away. He fires his gun, and a flash of fear comes over you. You believe he will shoot you if he catches you.

He is not going to give up. You think he might track you all the way to Simone's cottage, which would be a disaster. You can't put all those other hidden children at risk. Even if he catches you, at least the rest will be safe. You dart off the path and into a thicket of bushes to hide.

After what must be an hour or more, you no longer hear the man. Your face is pocked with mosquito bites, and you gently raise your hand to scratch. It's the first you have moved even an inch in a long time.

TO STAY HIDDEN FOR A BIT LONGER, TURN TO PAGE 61.

TO QUIETLY GET BACK ON THE PATH AND KEEP GOING, TURN TO PAGE 62.

57

You stop, and the Soldier steps into your path. The sleeves of his uniform are rolled up, revealing very hairy arms. He licks the lips of his large, wolfish grin.

"Where are you going?" he asks again.

"Just to my grandmother's house," you reply. "She is ill and I'm bringing her some cake to cheer her up."

The Soldier strokes his long beard. Then he says, "And where does your grandmother live?"

You step away. The Soldier steps closer. He draws his pistol.

"Tell me where she lives," he says, "or I will shoot you. And don't lie, child. I can tell when children lie."

The way he looks at you with those big, yellow eyes, you wouldn't be surprised if he *can* tell when children lie. Soldiers are well-trained interrogators. Maybe you can tell him a partial truth and run ahead to Bon Jardin to warn Simone. At least then you'd have a chance of surviving.

TO LIE AND GIVE HIM A FALSE LOCATION, TURN TO PAGE 63.

TO TELL HIM A PARTIAL TRUTH ABOUT THE TOWN OF BON JARDIN, TURN TO PAGE 64.

You rest your head on your knees. Soon you hear footsteps coming. You were right to stay hidden! As he approaches, your fear increases and you struggle to calm your breathing. A raccoon stumbles through the brush near you, and the Soldier shines his light in your direction. When he sees the raccoon, he sweeps the light back toward the path. That was close.

But he doesn't keep walking. He stands on the path listening. Or is he smelling the air? He gazes all around as if he can sense that you are near. A fruit bat swoops across the path.

You realize that your red cape and hood are bright—easy to see if the light hits them. For a moment the Soldier turns away from you to look down the path toward your home village.

TO REMOVE THE CAPE AND HOOD AND STAY HIDDEN, TURN TO PAGE 66.

TO GET UP AND RUN, TURN TO PAGE 68.

You step gingerly out of the brush, carefully avoiding any twigs that might snap underfoot. You crouch low for a few seconds, but you don't sense any movement. Perhaps he's really gone.

You start back on the path toward Bon Jardin, only now you are running. You've been hiding a long time, and dawn will come soon. As you run, your breathing echoes in your head, and your own footfalls begin to sound very loud. Your mind is playing tricks on you.

You stop and listen. You can't be sure, but you think you hear the Soldier's footsteps some distance behind you. Better keep running—you can't waste any more time hiding or you'll be caught in the daylight.

TURN TO PAGE 68.

You'd rather risk lying than put Simone and the other children in danger. "She lives in the town," you say, pointing back toward your own village. "I was just picking some berries for her."

The Soldier reaches down and lifts you by your red hood. Your feet dangle in the air. His breath smells like a dead animal. He holds his pistol in front of you.

"You shouldn't have tested me," he says and knocks you on the head with his pistol. When you wake up, your hands are tied together and he is dragging you by the hood along the path. You don't know what will happen to you, but it won't be good. You try to take comfort in the fact that you didn't give up Simone and the other children. At least they still have a chance.

63

THE END

TO FOLLOW ANOTHER PATH, TURN TO PAGE 9.

"She lives in Bon Jardin," you say.

"Strange time to be visiting," the Soldier says.

"She's very sick," you say. "She's all alone. I was worried."

"Where in Bon Jardin does she live?"

"She runs an inn on the main road," you lie.

"Very well," he says and lets go of your hood. You step away from him. When he doesn't follow, you turn to run down the path.

After more than two hours, you arrive in the village, sweating and exhausted. You see the cottage, just as father described. Two large brown trucks are parked nearby. As you approach the door to the cottage, you hear voices inside arguing. A woman is sobbing.

Down the road you see Soldiers escorting a line of children from a schoolhouse. Despair fills your heart. The Soldiers found them. It's all your fault. In worrying about your own safety, you betrayed a whole village and the hundreds of children hidden here.

You turn to find a Soldier standing behind you. He orders you to join the other children being loaded onto the trucks.

THE END

TO FOLLOW ANOTHER PATH, TURN TO PAGE 9.

Carefully you untie the string at your throat. You pull the hood and cape off slowly. As you lean onto your side to hide the garment under your legs, you put your hand on a thorny branch. Before you can think, you cry out—a short yip of pain.

The Soldier turns and shines his lantern in your direction. You remain perfectly still.

The Soldier steps closer to you. "Come out, child," he says.

You hold your breath.

"Show yourself, now!" he barks.

Your heart thumps and your hands tremble. Suddenly his flashlight is in your eyes, and you're blinded. Branches and brush crack as he tramples toward you. The light gets brighter, suddenly recedes, and then comes flashing back as he brings the flashlight down on your head with a clunk.

You come to with a horrible headache. You groan and roll over. "Get up," the Soldier says.

He ties your hands and leads you stumbling back toward your own village. He takes you to the train station and loads you into a big car with dozens of other children. You're so scared you throw up on your shirt. You have heard of these train cars. Children taken away on them do not come back. All around you, people are crying. A boy you know is calling out the names of his sisters and brothers, but no one is answering.

You close your eyes and cry too.

67

THE END

TO FOLLOW ANOTHER PATH, TURN TO PAGE 9.

You've never run so fast or so far in your life. You keep running until you emerge from the woods, exhausted. It's morning—the sky is blue and birds chirp in the trees. Up ahead you see a small home. It must be Simone's cottage. Farther along the street you see a church, a schoolhouse, and more homes.

You hurry to the cottage and knock.

"Come in," says a gruff voice from inside.

It doesn't sound like a woman's voice, but you open the door and lean your head in. At first you don't see anyone. From another room comes the voice again. "Come in here, to the bedroom."

Things don't seem right, so before coming in you grab the shovel that is leaning near the door. Your whole body is on edge. From the bedroom come the sounds of furniture sliding on the floor and then a loud thud.

"Run!" a woman's voice screams. You hear someone being hit hard, and then the Soldier comes out of the room.

TO RUN OUT THE DOOR, **TURN TO PAGE 70.**

TO TRY TO SAVE SIMONE, **TURN TO PAGE 72.**

You drop the shovel and run from the cottage with the Soldier chasing after. You leap down the porch stairs and nearly run into a tall man with a long robe and beard—and a rifle aimed right at you.

Bang!

You collapse to the ground and cover your ears. When you look up, you see the Soldier lying dead behind you, blood trickling from a hole in his chest.

"Come with me," says the man with the rifle. "I said come on!" he shouts, grabbing your arm.

The man is a pastor. He brings you back into Simone's cottage where she is tied up in the bedroom. He frees her and then says, "Get the child into hiding, fast."

While the pastor drags the Soldier's body out of sight, Simone takes you out a back door, across a wide lawn, through a graveyard, and into another woods. Pulling you by the arm, she takes you deep into the trees and asks you to crawl into a hole under a tree root. She covers the hole with branches and leaves.

"Don't come out, don't make any sound, until I come for you," Simone says.

She leaves and it is silent. You are terrified but grateful to have found Simone. A long time passes before you hear voices nearby.

"Come out now, children!" says a deep voice. You don't think it is the pastor, but you can't be sure. "It's okay," he says. "Come on out. Hurry!"

TO CLIMB OUT OF YOUR HOLE, TURN TO PAGE 73.

TO STAY HIDDEN, TURN TO PAGE 74.

Simone is in danger. You can't just leave her, so you grip the shovel hard and stand your ground. The Soldier closes in, baring his yellow teeth in an evil smile.

"My, what big teeth you've got," you say before swinging the shovel. You hit him in the face, and his smile vanishes.

He pulls his pistol from its holster and points it at you. Feeling like you have nothing to lose, you swing the shovel again, hitting his arm just as he fires. The bullet shatters a window behind you. The pistol drops to the floor.

72

You've never fired a gun before, but it may be your best chance to escape. Can you get to it before the Soldier does? Maybe you should just whack him with the shovel again.

TO REACH FOR THE GUN, TURN TO PAGE 76.

TO HIT HIM WITH THE SHOVEL, TURN TO PAGE 77.

Simone said not to come out until she called for you, but perhaps she sent someone else. You push the brush away and peer around, hoping to see the pastor. Instead you see a Soldier pointing a rifle at you. Behind him stand a dozen other uniformed men.

"Here's one," the Soldier calls out. "I'd bet everything I have that there are more." He grabs your arm and twists it. A bolt of pain wrenches through you. He cuffs your wrists together behind your back. It hurts so much you think you might faint.

"They're hiding dozens of children out here." 73
The men clear brush away from other holes. You lock eyes with another child who's been pulled from her hiding spot. You share a look of terror.

THE END

TO FOLLOW ANOTHER PATH, TURN TO PAGE 9.

Simone said to stay hidden until she came for you, so that's what you do. You hear heavy boots crunching through the brush, and you hold your breath.

Finally the forest is silent again. You keep waiting. Daylight has faded to night by the time Simone shines a lantern above your hole. "It's okay," she says.

Around you in the forest, you see dozens of other children climbing out of holes. Amazing. You had no idea all these hiding places were here.

74

Simone and the pastor take you and the others into the schoolhouse. You sit at desks while they bring soup, bread, and cheese from a kitchen. You realize you're starving, and you eat greedily.

All the children are housed in a room above the schoolhouse. Over the next few weeks, Pastor Michel visits often to teach lessons. Sometimes he tells you stories about his rescue missions. He leaves at night, sneaks through the forest, and leads frightened children to safety at his schoolhouse.

Months go by, and the Soldiers have not come back. You feel restless. You are one of the older children, and you want to help Pastor Michel on his rescue missions. It would be a way to thank him and Simone and help save other kids. When you think of children being hunted by those hairy Soldiers, it gives you the shivers.

75

On the other hand, maybe what gives you the shivers is the idea of the Soldiers out there looking for *you*.

TO STAY WITH SIMONE, WHERE YOU FEEL MOST SAFE, TURN TO PAGE 79.

TO ASK PASTOR MICHEL IF YOU CAN HELP HIM, TURN TO PAGE 80.

You dive onto the gun and feel its cold steel in your hand for a split second before hearing a loud crack. You touch your head and your hand comes back wet with blood. You realize the crack was the sound of your skull being hit with something. A strange sensation spreads through your body. You look across the floor at the legs of Simone's bed and suddenly feel sleepy and dizzy.

The Soldier pushes you over with his boot, and you roll easily. The gun is no longer in your hand. Did you let it go on purpose? Why did you want it? It's so hard to remember.

76

As the Soldier picks it up and points it at you, you manage to focus on his face for a second. "My, what big eyes you have," the man says with a snarl as he closes in. Then the world goes black.

THE END

TO FOLLOW ANOTHER PATH, TURN TO PAGE 9.

You can't easily reach the gun. But the Soldier goes for it. You bring the blade of the shovel down hard on his forearm, snapping it at an unnatural angle. The Soldier howls in pain.

A shadow fills the door of the cottage behind you. You turn to see a tall man in a black robe standing with a rifle at his shoulder. You shut your eyes, and the gun goes off. You hear the Soldier collapse, and his howling stops.

TURN THE PAGE.

When you open your eyes again, the Soldier is lying dead a few inches from you.

"I'm Pastor Michel," the man says.

You spend the next several months living in the schoolhouse with the other children. You must hide in the woods when Soldiers come looking. But you are never caught. You owe your life to Simone and the pastor, and to your parents, who sent you away to save you.

THE END

TO FOLLOW ANOTHER PATH, TURN TO PAGE 9.

As much as you want to help, it seems too risky. You stay and try to keep your hopes up.

Sometimes Soldiers return to search again. A communication system has been set up in the village to warn Simone when trouble is coming. The children are rushed out to hide in the woods before the Soldiers arrive. You become special friends with another student at the school who smiles at you in a way that is different from the others. The smiles make you feel a little less lonely.

When the war ends, you are old enough to start your own family. You marry your smiling friend from the school. Many years later, it makes your heart seize with sadness—but also joy—when you watch your own children play hide-and-seek in the woods.

79

THE END

TO FOLLOW ANOTHER PATH, TURN TO PAGE 9.

Pastor Michel says he has noticed your courage, skill, and desire. He is as grateful for your help as you are for his.

One night he takes you out onto the trail leading back toward your home village. Pastor Michel has learned that a little girl is fleeing through these woods, just as you did so long ago.

You find the girl alone in the bushes near the same spot where you had hidden from the Soldier in your red cape and hood. Your escape is a distant memory, like it happened in another lifetime. The wide-eyed girl is trembling. Pastor Michel reaches a hand for her, but she turns away. You crouch down to the girl's level.

80

"This is a good hiding spot," you tell her. "We never would have found you, except that I used it myself one time. I hid from one of those mean Soldiers and got away. I guess you and I have something in common—smarts."

You talk to the girl for a little while, and gradually she looks into your face. She's still trembling. There's no telling what horror she has seen. But she decides she trusts you, and you lead her out of the woods to safety.

Over the next few months, you rescue many more children. You have a couple close calls, but you are never caught. By the end of the war, you have become a hero to many.

81

THE END

TO FOLLOW ANOTHER PATH, TURN TO PAGE 9.

CHAPTER 4

Attack Plans

You are a special agent working in the Resistance against FocusHood, the corrupt corporation ruling your continent. FocusHood is trying to stamp out all creativity. Creativity leads to inefficiency and to people doing things for fun—or worse, for love—instead of for the State. But creativity, fun, and love are things that you believe in. That is why you took the risk of joining the Resistance.

FocusHood started as a software company that designed a program to increase productivity. Soon the company developed a hood that blocked out all distractions. Wearing the hood made people 100 percent efficient.

Soon FocusHood owned every company on the continent. Every store, every job, every park, every bit of food was owned by FocusHood—even the government.

Especially the government. The police and trained wolves are now constantly on the lookout for those who don't wear FocusHoods, to force them to do so. You have heard that the hoods will brainwash you into being a slave to the State of FocusHood, which is what your continent is now called.

You are carrying plans, hidden in a cake inside a basket, to Special Agent Grandma (Agent Granny). She's a very important figure in the Resistance. FocusHood would love to imprison her. The information you carry describes an attack plan on one of Focushood's factories. You wear a red cape and hood that is designed to look like a FocusHood but is really just a plain hood.

You were almost through the woods when you heard a voice. Now you hear the voice again: "Where are you going, child?" It is a wolf.

"I am focused on my job," you say, as you have been instructed to do. "I'm delivering this cake to a customer." The wolf looks in the basket, sniffs, and strokes his chin. He says you can pass. You walk away, but you feel like you are still being watched. Is the wolf following you? You turn back but you see nothing.

Ahead of you the path splits in two directions. The right fork leads to Agent Granny's, and you're in a hurry. But if the wolf follows you, you'll lead him right to her. You're not sure where the left fork goes, but at least taking it won't reveal Agent Granny's location.

TO TAKE THE RIGHT FORK TO AGENT GRANNY'S HOUSE, TURN TO PAGE 86.

TO TAKE THE LEFT FORK, TURN TO PAGE 87.

There isn't any time to spare, so you hurry down the right path, out of the woods, and directly to Agent Granny's.

Agent Granny lives in a plain brown house on a street full of plain brown houses. You know which one is hers because the mailbox has a tiny red splotch of paint on it—a subtle sign to rebel agents.

When you knock on the door, a voice invites you to come in, but it sounds gravelly. You've never spoken with Agent Granny, so you don't know what she sounds like. If you don't deliver the plans, the attack will probably fail. On the other hand, if a wolf has found her, the plan will definitely fail.

TO WALK IN, TURN TO PAGE 88.

TO LEAVE WITH THE ATTACK PLANS, TURN TO PAGE 90.

You can't risk leading the wolf to Agent Granny's house, so you dodge down the left trail. Through the trees you see more eyes looking at you—more wolves! They're everywhere.

You keep going, turning here and there trying to lose them, but soon *you're* lost. You sit down to catch your breath, and you feel the wolves all around you. Down the path, you see a light. As it bobs closer to you, a human figure takes shape. A headlamp shines from beneath the man's hood. He's carrying an electro-blaster gun.

The wolves duck deeper into the trees as the man approaches. It is hard to tell the color of his hood with his light shining on you, but you think it might be red.

"Come with me," he says, kind but urgent.

87

TO FOLLOW HIM, TURN TO PAGE 91.

TO STAY, TURN TO PAGE 92.

This is no time to be afraid—the Resistance is depending on you. You step inside. Someone in a red hood is sitting on a chair facing away from you. A big, hairy hand holds a thick book.

"Agent Granny," you say nervously. "What big hands you've got."

"The better to work with," the figure says. "And speaking of work, I believe you have something for me," the voice continues.

You're suspicious. "What's the password?" you ask. A low growl comes from under the hood. It makes the hair on your neck stiffen. "That's not the password, Granny."

If it's the wolf, then what happened to Agent Granny? She's a legendary hero! If the wolf was able to destroy her, there's no telling what he would do to you.

You back up to the door. "Leave the plans, child," rumbles the voice.

89

TO LEAVE THE PLANS AND RUN FOR YOUR LIFE, TURN TO PAGE 94.

TO TAKE THE PLANS WITH YOU, TURN TO PAGE 96.

It's too risky. You don't trust that the voice was Agent Granny's. You turn and head down the street. There's a café nearby where you can hide in the crowd and call Resistance headquarters. Maybe they've heard something from Agent Granny. You walk through a plaza bustling with people wearing FocusHoods. They are rushing to work with no time to let their minds wander or notice the clouds.

Poor fools, you think. They are like robots. They don't know it, but you're going to save them.

You sit near the back of the café and call headquarters, but nobody answers. A red-caped man across the room catches your eye, but just then a waiter approaches your table. It's a wolf.

"Something to drink?" the wolf asks. Is it the same wolf from the woods? You can't tell.

TO ACT CASUAL AND ORDER A DRINK, TURN TO PAGE 98.

TO QUICKLY LEAVE THE CAFÉ, TURN TO PAGE 103.

90

The man knows his way through the woods, and soon you emerge near the edge of town. You walk across a parking lot toward a gas station. Inside, the man leads you behind the counter to an office, where another red-caped agent waits.

"I'm Peter," the man says, taking a seat behind the desk. "Agent Granny has been captured by the wolves. By now they likely have her in a FocusHood. She's probably brainwashed and … efficient!" He spits the last word. "Give me the plans," he says, and you hand over the basket. He reaches a finger into the middle of the cake and pulls out a flash drive sealed in plastic wrap.

91

"I'll get these plans to Agent Granny's faction. I need you two to rescue Granny."

TURN TO PAGE 100.

You don't know if you can trust this man. He might be an ally, but the plans you're carrying are too valuable to risk it. "No thank you," you say.

The man grabs your wrist. "Come on!" he says. "Time is short!"

In the woods off the path, a wolf slinks low to the ground, watching, waiting to see what will happen. The man notices too. He tries to grab your basket, but you hold tight. As the wolf approaches, the man takes a step back.

"What's the trouble?" the wolf asks.

"No trouble," the man says. "Just working efficiently."

"Be on your way then," the wolf says to the man. He holds out a paw that suggests you are not free to go.

The man looks at you one last time. "You should have come with me," he says as he walks away.

The wolf takes the basket from your hands and looks inside. "This cake looks very ... creative," he says, scraping some frosting off with his claw and licking it.

"That is how the customer ordered it," you say.

"Is that right?" the wolf asks. Suddenly he grabs you by the arms and throws you over his shoulder. "We'll just take you in to make sure your FocusHood is working properly."

You are about to be fitted with a real **93** FocusHood and will lose all your creativity and desire for fun. Worse yet, the plans in will be discovered. You have let down the Resistance.

THE END

TO FOLLOW ANOTHER PATH, TURN TO PAGE 9.

You run all the way back to headquarters. All around you, people in FocusHoods are on their way to work, tapping on their devices as they walk. Some are conducting meetings over the phone: "5%." "No deal!" "Deliver by Tuesday!" No making plans for the weekend or discussing last night's TV. Never distracted.

You reach headquarters, hidden in the basement of another brown house, naturally. You use your key card to gain entrance, then head down to the basement hideout. Resistance workers are watching surveillance screens and discussing attack plans.

Your boss, Big Mama, rushes over and hugs you. "What happened?" she asks, looking unhappy. She's holding a device up to her ear, listening to a report.

"What do you mean?" you ask.

"FocusHood wolf agents have intercepted the plans. Were you attacked by a wolf? Are you okay?"

"I left the plans with Agent Granny …" you say. But you know you made a terrible mistake leaving the plans there. That was no grandma.

Big Mama listens again to the device. "Oh, no," she says. Others in the room stop what they're doing and turn to look. "They've traced the plans to us," Big Mama says. "They're coming."

You hang your red hood in shame. You realize **95** that in order to restore creativity, fun, and love, you must first be brave.

THE END

TO FOLLOW ANOTHER PATH, TURN TO PAGE 9.

You tuck the basket under your arm and run. "Come back!" the voice calls after you.

On the street, a wolf slips out from behind a car and starts chasing you, claws clicking on the hard pavement. You dash into a narrow alley where you toss the basket into a trash bin and keep running. You'll come back for it later.

When you emerge from the alley on the other side, the wolf is waiting. How did he get there so fast? Or maybe it's another wolf. They're teaming up!

The second wolf grabs you by the shoulders, and you try to fight him off. You catch a glimpse of the first wolf fishing for the basket in the trash. You're thrown to the ground, and your head is ringing as you see the wolf lean over you with gleaming teeth.

But then you hear a zap, and the wolf collapses beside you.

A tall red-caped man carrying an electro-blaster dashes up. "We have to get that cake back!" he says and runs toward the wolf that is still garbage diving. You're not sure you're up for more encounters with teeth and claws.

TO FOLLOW THE MAN WITH THE BLASTER AND FIGHT THE OTHER WOLF FOR THE BASKET, TURN TO PAGE 101.

TO ESCAPE WHILE YOU CAN, TURN TO PAGE 102.

You order a glass of milk from the wolf. The man in the red hood sips water and watches you.

When the wolf waiter is gone, you call headquarters again. Big Mama answers. "What's going on?" she asks. "Have you delivered the cake?"

You explain about the wolf's voice at Agent Granny's house.

Big Mama laughs. "No wolf can defeat Agent Granny," she says. "Go back and bring her the cake. She's waiting for you."

You leave a few coins on the table and dash out without your milk. As you jog back toward Agent Granny's house, you notice that the caped man from the café is following you. Many people in red hoods are allies—that is a signal to each other. But you can't be sure.

TO GO ON TO AGENT GRANNY'S HOUSE, GO TO PAGE 99.

TO CONFRONT THE MAN, TURN TO PAGE 103.

You ignore the man and continue on to Agent Granny's. When you knock, a raspy voice tells you to come in.

"Now give me the plans," a drooling creature demands as you enter. Big Mama was wrong—it *is* the wolf. You turn to run, but a second wolf stops you. "I've got a nice hood for you," he says.

Later, in a sterile room, you are strapped to a table. A wolf approaches and places a black hood over your head. A feeling you can only describe as electric honey oozes through your brain.

You experience a brief flash of terror as you feel all your human desires well up and then begin to slip away. The wolf watches the screen above you and murmurs, "My, what big dreams you had …"

99

THE END

TO FOLLOW ANOTHER PATH, TURN TO PAGE 9.

You and a scruffy-faced agent named Dogface Bob sneak by foot toward a prison across town. You have intelligence that Agent Granny is in a holding cell near the gates. Dogface Bob is a highly trained combat veteran. The plan is for him to fight the guards while you cut the power on the electric gates and free Agent Granny.

But as you approach the prison gate, Dogface Bob turns to look at you with cold, yellow eyes. His hood slips down, revealing a hairy neck and long, dripping teeth. A wolf! You turn to run, but he knocks you to the ground. You're taken inside the prison and down a long, cold hallway to a cell where one other person sits alone: Agent Granny.

"Enjoy your last night of free thought, humans," hisses Dogface Bob.

THE END

TO FOLLOW ANOTHER PATH, TURN TO PAGE 9.

The man runs down the alley. You follow. By now the wolf has pulled your basket from the trash and is running in the other direction. The man aims his blaster and shoots. The wolf goes rigid then tips to the ground like a falling tree. The basket clatters onto the street. You grab it.

Later, at a secret base, you and the man deliver the plans to Granny herself, who escaped to safety there. That night you help execute the attack perfectly. You shut down the remote power controls at one of FocusHood's largest factories. Afterward, as you walk home in the early morning light, you hear something. It's a person whistling a tune. You realize you haven't heard anyone whistle—or sing or laugh—in many months. You smile and whistle too.

THE END

TO FOLLOW ANOTHER PATH, TURN TO PAGE 9.

As the man runs into the alley aiming his blaster at the wolf, you head for the forest. But when you hear another zap, you stop to see what happened.

A second later the man appears, breathing hard. "The wolf got away with the plans," he yells. Now the Corporation will know what the Resistance is up to."

But you quickly realize that is the least of your worries. Six wolves slip out from between the trees and come toward you. There is no point in resisting.

That night you are fitted with a FocusHood. You feel the needs to love and create evaporate from your heart. In their place is the desire to work. Your first job, fed from the Corporation directly into your brain, is simple: Find Agent Granny and destroy her.

You know you will do it with great efficiency.

THE END

TO FOLLOW ANOTHER PATH, TURN TO PAGE 9.

You glance over your shoulder and see that the red-caped man is right behind you. "Why are you following me?" you ask.

He whispers, "Follow me. I'm here to help you!" You're not sure if you believe him, but you follow him to Granny's hideout. At the door a tall wrinkly woman greets the man, calling him Peter. "This is our new agent," Peter says, gesturing toward you. She reaches for her glasses and asks you for the plans.

Gathering your courage, you ask, "What is the password?"

Granny looks at you, impressed. "Well done," she nods and answers: "Crimson."

The three of you look at the plans while you lick frosting off your fingers. Agent Granny makes a few phone calls. The attack for that night is on.

TURN THE PAGE.

Agent Granny is a wild driver. She careens through the city streets, trying to get to the FocusHood factory in time to drive through the security gate, which Peter will be opening in less than two minutes.

You arrive and see a fire blazing, as planned. You drive right by it and glide through the gate, which lifts just in time. Three other agents tumble out of the van and go on a wolf hunt. It's your job to scale the building and slip into a window on the fifth floor. Once inside, you lock the door to the room and find the main computer server.

But some wolves have found you too. You hear claws scratching at the door and the whimpers of animals desperate for meat.

Quickly you slip the pin out of your cape, which holds a secret flash drive. You insert the drive into the computer just as the wolves crash through the door, claws glinting in the soft glow of the computer screens. Instantly there is a popping sound. Lights all over the city flicker, and the wolves drop from their hind legs to all-fours. They look at you with confusion, then slink away, tails between their legs.

The attack was a success! You meet up with the others and return to headquarters. Along the way you see people newly freed from their FocusHoods, looking at the stars in a daze. Four more factory attacks like this and you will have deactivated all the FocusHoods in the State.

But you'll have to be efficient.

THE END

TO FOLLOW ANOTHER PATH, TURN TO PAGE 9.

CHAPTER 5

A Little History on Little Red

The story that eventually became "Little Red Riding Hood" was told orally long before anyone wrote it down. Researchers believe that the story may have evolved from a tale told in Europe and the Middle East in the 1st century. This story, "The Wolf and the Kids," featured a nanny goat who warns her kids not to open the door while she is out. A wolf overhears her and tricks the kids into letting him in. He then eats them up.

By the 10th century, French peasants were telling a tale closer to the one we know today. A priest wrote it as a poem in Latin in the 11th century, and it spread to Austria and Italy.

The early versions didn't always have a wolf as the villain. Sometimes it was an ogre or a werewolf. The girl did not wear a red riding hood yet. But the main elements—a girl carrying treats to her grandmother and a villain who tricks her—were in place. There was no male adult to help the girl, though she usually escaped on her own.

In the 1600s French author Charles Perrault wrote the first published version of the story. He introduced the red cape and hood and named the girl Little Red Riding Hood. In Perrault's version the girl does not escape—she is eaten by the wolf! In case readers didn't quite understand the meaning of the story, he added a moral to the end: Children should not talk to strangers.

The Brothers Grimm wrote their version of the story in the 1800s. They added the huntsman, who bursts into the cottage and saves Little Red Riding Hood and her grandmother. The brothers even wrote a sequel in which Red and her grandmother wise up. When a wolf tries to trick them again, the grandmother locks the door to keep him out. Then she and Red cook sausages in a pot over a fire. The smell attracts the wolf, who climbs down the chimney and is boiled in the pot.

Today most people are familiar with the Grimms' version of "Little Red Riding Hood." Many creators have fun putting their own spin on it. Author Roald Dahl published a humorous poetic version in 1982, and Little Red has been retold and adapted in many other modern forms.

An animated movie called *Hoodwinked!* came out in 2005. A comical retelling of the tale, the movie centers around a police investigation of the Big Bad Wolf's crime.

CRITICAL THINKING
USING THE COMMON CORE

⚜ In Chapter 5 the author talks about the "moral" in Charles Perrault's version of "Little Red Riding Hood." What is meant by "the moral of the story"? What is the moral that Perrault's version emphasized? (Craft and Structure)

⚜ This book offers three different perspectives from the character of Little Red Riding Hood. How might the stories be different if they were told from the wolf's or villain's point of view? (Key Ideas and Details)

⚜ Imagine your own Red Riding Hood story. What is the setting? How would the characters and plot be different from the original tale? Would your tale have a moral? (Integration of Knowledge and Ideas)

READ MORE

Bradman, Tony. *Red Riding Hood Takes Charge.*
North Mankato: Stone Arch Books, 2009.

Doherty, Berlie. *Classic Fairy Tales: Candlewick Illustrated
Classic.* Somerville, Mass.: Candlewick Press, 2009.

Frampton, Otis. *Red Riding Hood, Superhero: A Graphic Novel.*
North Mankato: Stone Arch Books, 2015.

INTERNET SITES

Use FactHound to find Internet sites related to this book.
All of the sites on FactHound have been researched by our staff.

Here's all you do:

Visit *www.facthound.com*

Type in this code: 9781491458563